MYSTIC ADVENTURES

JOURNEYS BEYOND THE KNOWN

NEEL MUKADAM

To those who find joy in the mysterious and magic in the unknown—this book is for you. For every curious mind that loves a good thrill and every heart that beats a little faster at the thought of adventure. May these stories spark your imagination and remind you that the most enchanting journeys often begin with a single step into the unknown.

Contents

Contents

Foreword

Hey there,

Thank you for picking up "Mystic Adventures." As you dive into these pages, I hope you're ready for a journey filled with excitement, mystery, and a bit of the supernatural. This book is a collection of stories where the everyday merges with the extraordinary, and where adventure lurks around every corner.

Writing these tales has been a real joy for me. Each story started with a simple idea and grew into something magical. I wanted to create a space where you can let your imagination run wild and experience the thrill of the unknown right alongside the characters.

I hope these stories capture your curiosity and transport you to places where wonder and adventure await. Thanks for joining me on this journey. I'm excited for you to explore and enjoy every twist and turn!

Happy reading!

Preface

Welcome to "Mystic Adventures"! This book is a collection of stories that take you on a journey through mystery, excitement, and the unknown. Each tale is a little adventure in itself, filled with unexpected twists and turns that I hope will keep you intrigued and entertained.

In "Forest Adventure: A Tale of Discovery and Danger," you'll find yourself in the depths of a mysterious forest, where surprises lurk at every corner. "Castle of Evil Dead" takes you to a haunted castle with a dark past, while "Underworld Secrets" dives into a hidden world beneath our feet.

"USA: My Beloved Motherland" is a heartfelt story that explores the beauty and diversity of a land close to my heart. You'll also encounter tales of justice and resilience in "Justice Triumphs: The Inspiring Story" and "One Day When Justice is Delivered," where truth and fairness come out on top.

"The Handkerchief's Secret" reveals a hidden story behind an ordinary object, while "The Dead House" and "Shadows of the Dancing Man" bring a touch of the eerie and supernatural. In "Robot Human," we explore the fascinating intersection of humanity and technology.

"Locked in Vegas: A Tale of Unexpected Friendship" shows how surprising friendships can form in the most unlikely places. "The Path from Struggle to Success" and "Light of Change: A Lighthouse's Lesson" offer stories of perseverance and transformation, inspiring us to keep going even when times are tough.

For the foodies, "The Search for Jack's Tasty Food" is a fun quest for culinary delight. And for those who love a good scare, "Don't Dare to Go into the Cave" and "Treasure Island - A Trap" promises thrilling adventures with a twist.

"Love, Betrayal, and Redemption" delves into the complexities of relationships and emotions, while "The Mystery of the Salford Cruise" sets sail on a sea of suspense and intrigue. Finally, "The Tale of the Serbian Dancing Lady" is a story filled with tradition, mystery, and a touch of the supernatural.

Each of these stories has a special place in my heart, and I hope they capture your imagination and bring a sense of adventure into your day. Thank you for joining me on this journey. I can't wait for you to dive into these tales and explore the mysteries within!

Enjoy the read!

Acknowledgements

Creating "Mystic Adventures" has been a rewarding journey, and I owe my deepest gratitude to the people who have supported me along the way.

First and foremost, I want to thank my parents. To my mother, who not only served as my editor but also offered invaluable guidance and encouragement throughout the writing process—your insights and meticulous attention to detail have been instrumental in bringing these stories to life. And to my father, whose life and wisdom have always been a source of inspiration—your strength and stories have shaped my imagination and fueled my passion for writing. Thank you for believing in me and for being my constant pillar of support.

A special thank you to my grandmother, whose love and wisdom have always been a comforting presence. Your warmth and stories have been a source of inspiration and joy. Thank you for nurturing my curiosity and for being a cherished part of my life.

To my friends and extended family, thank you for your unwavering encouragement and for always being there to cheer me on. Your love and support have meant the world to me. To my readers, both old and new, your enthusiasm and feedback have been incredibly motivating. I hope these stories bring you the same joy and excitement that I felt while writing them.

Finally, a heartfelt thank you to all the storytellers and dreamers who have inspired me with their tales. Your creativity and imagination have sparked my own, and I am grateful to be a part of this wonderful world of storytelling.

ACKNOWLEDGEMENTS

Thank you all for being a part of this adventure. Your support and love have made "Mystic Adventures" possible.

Prologue

As the day turns into night and the world grows quiet, a different kind of magic begins. In these quiet moments, anything seems possible. Welcome to "Mystic Adventures," a collection of stories where the ordinary becomes extraordinary, and each tale holds a new adventure.

In this book, you'll explore haunted places, hidden worlds, and heartfelt journeys. You'll meet characters who face challenges, discover secrets, and sometimes encounter the supernatural. These stories are about the thrill of discovering the unknown, the quest for justice, the joy of unexpected friendships, and the ups and downs of love and betrayal.

Every story offers a glimpse into a different world, where things are not always as they seem. As you read, let your imagination wander. Whether you're in the mood for excitement, mystery, or a thoughtful moment, these tales are here to take you on a special journey.

So, get ready to explore. The world of "Mystic Adventures" is waiting for you. The adventure begins now.

CHAPTER ONE

Forest Adventure: A Tale of Discovery and Danger

In a peaceful little village surrounded by hills and green woods, my cousin Frank and I went on an adventure that changed our lives. We were on a mission to visit my uncle, Mr. Aniston, who lived in a strange house full of mysteries.

As we journeyed deeper into the forest, Frank got a bit worried and asked, "Are you sure this is the right way to reach Mr. Aniston's place?" I nodded with determination. Mr. Aniston was my uncle. I'd only heard stories about it, and his peculiar house had always fascinated me.

Our journey led us to a peculiarly shaped house and my cousin couldn't help but wonder and ask, "Is this Mr. Aniston's house?" I didn't say anything and knocked on the door. A man with curly hair opened it and asked, "What brings you here, my boy?" I confidently said, "Uncle, we have come to live with you. This is my cousin, Frank Black." Mr. Aniston welcomed us warmly, and we sat down at a table inside. Little did we know that our adventure would take a surprising and dangerous turn. Suddenly, a huge white rabbit hopped into the room, surprising and confusing us. I was surprised after seeing such a big rabbit but Mr. Aniston said, he is my pet. Frank couldn't contain his amazement, "Where did you find such a huge rabbit?" Frank asked. But before we could understand what was happening, the rabbit jumped on Frank, knocking him down.

Mr. Aniston immediately called out, "Cyber, come back!" Yet, Cyber, the rabbit, appeared to be driven by an unseen force as it disappeared into the forest, carrying my cousin away with it. Fear pushed me to run after them, determined to save Frank. But the forest swallowed them whole, leaving me alone with my worry. Aniston, too, went into the forest to search for them, leaving me to face the uncertainty within the house. I was alone in the Aniston's house. As I went inside, the outside world faded, and my heart pounded with uncertainty. Then, I heard a noise behind me. Without warning, a ferocious tiger leaped towards me, and fear gripped me tightly. My vision blurred, and everything went dark.

When I finally woke up and opened my eyes, found myself lying in a hospital bed, feeling disoriented and weak. I sat up and asked in a trembling voice, "Who saved me?" It was Mr. Aniston who stood by my side, his eyes filled with sadness. "You were very close to death," he explained gently. "The tiger had bitten you, and you had a heart attack. Your heart had stopped beating."

I was amazed, grappling with the realization that I had come dangerously close to death and somehow come back. Aniston continued, his voice heavy with sorrow, "I'm sorry to say that your cousin, Frank, didn't make it. My rabbit, Cyber, was responsible for his tragic end."

I was overwhelmed with sorrow, realizing the high cost of our adventure into the mysterious house in the forest. It had been a journey filled with mysteries and, sadly, heartbreaking loss, something we would never forget.

As days turned into weeks, I couldn't help but frequently reflect on Frank and the unusual things that had happened. These experiences taught me the importance of being careful and how much family means.

Mr. Aniston, who had gone through the same difficult times as me, became more than just a friend; he was like a second father. Our lives took a sharp turn, and we both discovered comfort in each other's presence. It was encouraging to know that even though we had faced tragedy, we had also created a strong, unbreakable connection.

****

CHAPTER TWO

Treasure Island- A trap

Once upon a time, in a cosy house, Uncle Sean, a man with a passion for adventures, planned a trip to a mysterious island. Little did he know that this adventure would turn into a big mystery.

"Oh dear, it's a trap!" Uncle Sean shouted with urgency; his eyes wide in alarm. Don and Ron, the two brave nephews, stared ahead and spotted a mysterious creature approaching them. What happened next was a mystery; they vanished without a trace, leaving everyone wondering where they could be.

Before this mysterious event, one day, Uncle Sean, a man of adventure, asked his kind-hearted wife, Rubia, "Can you make breakfast for my nephews"? Aunt Rubia, whose dream was to become a lawyer, agreed with a warm smile. However, Uncle Sean dismissed her dream. "While I am preparing your breakfast, you should do a cleaning of the floor," she said.

Uncle Sean agreed and went to take his broom. Ron, one of the brave nephews, helped him clean the floor, and for their hard work, Uncle Sean rewarded them with ten pennies. The air was filled with excitement when Uncle Sean declared, "We are going on an island!" Aunt Rubia wasn't thrilled about this adventure, though she didn't show it. She loved her nephews a lot.

Breakfast was served, and the nephews, full of excitement, asked, "Where are we going?" Aunt Rubia, in her frustration, replied, "Ask your uncle. This scoundrel won't tell me where we're going." An argument followed, and Aunt Rubia went to her room in tears.

Sean shouted at Rubia, explaining they were going to a treasure island to spend peaceful time, and if she had a problem with it, she should leave his house. A heated argument followed, and Rubia went to her room in tears. Uncle Sean was also unhappy after the argument with his wife. He went to apologize, but he got slapped and faced fierce words. Rubia said, "I am not coming with you to some unknown island."

Sean said, in a low voice, "I am sorry. You damaged my reputation. So, I have no option but to quarrel with you. Please forgive me and come with us." In the heat of the moment, Sean made a wrong decision, locking Rubia in her room.

Ron and Don were shocked and pleaded with Uncle Sean to be kind to Aunt Rubia. Instead, Sean punched Ron and shouted angrily, "You have no idea about my wife. She is an annoyance for me, and I can't handle her". Ron was hurt badly and unconscious. Don said, "Uncle, we have to take Ron to the hospital."

Don, realizing the severity, suggested taking Ron to the hospital, but Sean, fearing legal repercussions, opposed the idea. The situation escalated, leaving Don in a state of shock. Uncle Sean warned Don not to take Ron to the hospital, saying it was risky because Aunt Rubia could make a case against him. Don was sad and left to open the lock, but Sean hung him up, making everything more confusing.

Contrary to what everyone expected, Uncle Sean's actions weren't the main problem. A creature named Lostofur, half-man and half-creature turned out to be the real trouble. The island adventure took a dark turn when they encountered Forgin, a man connected to Lostofur.

A battle resulted, Sean ended up unconscious, and Ron and Don disappeared. Lostofur, the puppet master, revealed his malevolent intentions, kidnapping the two innocent boys, and leaving their fate hanging in the balance.

After 10 years

Ten long years passed, and the once lively house fell silent. The story unfolded in front of Ron and Don's parents, revealing the troubled past. Keith, Don's father, faced the harsh truth about his brother's behaviour and decided that justice must prevail.

Keith believed justice was more important than family ties, and punishment was necessary to fix the wrongs. The story of Treasure Island, once an exciting adventure, turned into a lesson about the consequences of hasty decisions and the dangers we can't always see.

****

CHAPTER THREE

Castle of Evil Dead

Once upon a time, a castle stood so spooky and eerie that even the bravest souls trembled at the mere thought of it. Its towering walls seemed to whisper horror and mystery tales, warning everyone who dared to approach. But despite the alarming warnings, my curiosity bubbled within me like a pot ready to boil over.

It all began with my grandmother, a wise old lady who loved to spin tales of the haunted castle. I was just a young boy then, barely ten years old, and the mere thought of the castle sent shivers down my spine. My grandmother often told me tales of the haunted castle that appeared ominously on the outskirts of our town. Despite her warnings, I was always too frightened to listen, preferring to block out the terrifying stories she spun.

One evening, as the sun dipped below the horizon, casting long shadows across the room, my grandmother began her usual tale of the castle's dark past. I could feel my heart racing as she described the ghostly spirits that roamed its halls and the eerie sounds that echoed through its corridors.

But fear got the better of me, and I refused to listen, burying my head under the covers to block out her words. Eventually, my grandmother sighed and finished her story, her voice shaded with sadness as she warned me never to go near the castle.

"Your grandfather went there once," she said solemnly, her eyes filled with sorrow. "And he never returned."

I shivered as her words sank in, understanding the gravity of her warning. With a trembling voice, I said, "I'm Monaro Flames, and I'm 10 years old." But even as I spoke, a sense of uneasiness washed over me, as if the castle's mysteries were signalling me to uncover the truth.

Ten years later, the memory of that story remained, haunting me. So, when my cousin Damos proposed an adventure to explore the northern part of America, I couldn't pass up the chance to oppose my fears.

After 10 years

Ten years had passed, and the attraction of adventure indicated once again. With my cousin Damos by my side, we boarded on a journey to explore the northern reaches of America. Our anticipation grew as we neared our destination, the landscape telling before us revealing an old, abandoned castle nestled among the rocky land. Its imposing silhouette against the darkening sky sent a shiver down my spine, but my cousin, unaware of any potential danger, stepped forth without hesitation. Ignoring my warnings, he crossed the threshold into the castle's eerie interior, his curiosity outweighing any sense of caution. Reluctantly, I followed, the weight of foreboding settling heavily upon me as we ventured deeper into the shadows that enveloped the ancient structure.

Inside the castle, it smelled musty and old, like things were rotting away. The sound of our footsteps echoed in the empty halls, making it feel like someone else was there with us. Even though the old building made creepy noises, my cousin kept going, excited to explore. As we went deeper, it got darker and harder to see, which made me feel uneasy. With each step, I couldn't shake the feeling that something spooky was waiting in the shadows and that the castle was hiding secrets that were creepier than we ever thought.

Danger in castle

The story of the Castle of Evil Dead took a chilling turn as we encountered a man with piercing brown eyes, the mysterious man inside who seemed to know more than he let on. His piercing brown eyes seemed to bore into our souls as he warned us to leave the castle. He warned us to leave, but my cousin's curiosity got the better of him. Ignoring his ominous words, my cousin pressed on, driven by his insatiable curiosity. Before we knew it, the man's threats grew more menacing, and we found ourselves fleeing from the castle in fear.

He asked what do you want? You know that no one dares to come here to explore this place. The man gave me an angry look and shouted you are Detective Mat Sheriffson, right? Get out of this castle. My frightened cousin attempted to reason with him, saying, "But my brother is just a simple man." Angered by our presence, the man shouted, "It doesn't matter if he is simple or complex. If you two don't leave this castle now, I will tear your flesh from your bones." Terrified, we quickly made our way out of the castle, eager to escape his madness. Desperate to escape, we fled from the castle, our hearts pounding with fear. But even as we left the castle behind, the sense of dread lingered, haunting us like a ghostly spectre.

Dead King's mystery

After leaving the spooky castle, my cousin and I felt a bit freaked out. He said the guy we met seemed nuts and dangerous, and I agreed. So, we decided to grab some food at Omo's Chicken Restaurant to calm our nerves.

But guess who we saw there? Yep, the same creepy guy from the castle, sitting all casual with a glass of wine. I tried to be friendly and offered him some wine, but he flipped out and threatened us. I got pretty mad and almost started a fight, but my brother and some other people stopped me. The restaurant manager told us to cool it and focus on eating.

After leaving the spooky castle, my cousin and I felt a bit freaked out. He said the guy we met seemed nuts and dangerous, and I agreed. So, we decided to grab some food at Omo's Chicken Restaurant to calm our nerves.

But guess who we saw there? Yep, the same creepy guy from the castle, sitting all casual with a glass of wine. I tried to be friendly and offered him some wine, but he flipped out and threatened us. I got pretty mad and almost started a fight, but my brother and some other people stopped me. The restaurant manager told us to cool it and focus on eating.

After dinner, we went for a walk to clear our heads. We didn't want to go back near the castle, so we took a different route. We went to a beautiful location and we thought of staying in the nearest hotel but we saw an old man coming towards us. He was holding a tombstone in his hand. My brother thought he was the same weirdo from the castle, but he wasn't. The old guy said his name was King Chris Bombando and claimed he was 550 years old, even though his tombstone said he died at 490. As we listened closely to the old man's stories, he leaned in and began to tell us about "The Mystery of the Old King." He said it was a story that had been around for ages, filled with secrets that nobody seemed to fully understand.

The old man explained that King Chris Bombando wasn't like other kings. He wasn't just a ruler of his kingdom; he was believed to be a guardian of ancient realms, responsible for keeping the balance between different worlds.

As we delved deeper into the conversation, we couldn't help but wonder how such longevity was possible. King Chris smiled knowingly, acknowledging the many theories that surrounded his remarkable lifespan. Some believed he had struck a deal with magical spirits, while others speculated about a hidden fountain of youth with mystical powers.

As the wind picked up, sending a chill down our spines, King Chris offered a word of caution. He warned us about the dangers of digging too deeply into secrets that were better left untouched. But despite the warning, the attraction of the old king's story had captured our imaginations, sparking a desire to uncover the truth, no matter the risks.

With a newfound sense of purpose, we offer farewell to King Chris, knowing that our journey is far from over. The mystery of the old king had burnt a flame of curiosity within us, driving us to seek out answers and board on an adventure filled with twists and turns, secrets waiting to be revealed, and dangers waiting in the shadows. And so, our mission for the truth began, guided by the mysterious tale of the castle of evil dead and the mysterious figure known as King Chris Bombando.

****

CHAPTER FOUR

USA: My Beloved Motherland

"Ok bro, I will call you later". Jacobson said to his patriot friend Arthur. A patriot is a civilian who takes pride in their own country. Arthur had an unwavering love for their beloved motherland, the USA. Jacobson was an exceptional special officer of the F.B.I., but he was a rebel and disliked obeying government rules. The biggest traitor to the USA was Bobby Sherolson who had a wife named Tamina. Long ago, Bobby was a very good actor, but one day his show flopped and the crowd said, "You don't deserve to act on this stage." Since that day Bobby started hating all the people of the USA. He developed a protest against his own country. His wife Tamina tried to console him, but the darkness in his heart only grew.

Jacobson knew this story and was very angry at the US public. Determined to change the perception, Jacobson decided to host to defend Bobby's talent. In this show, he said, "Just because one of your shows flopped doesn't mean Bobby is a bad actor. In this world, no one is perfect. Let us give my friend Bobby a chance to shine again." After the show, Jacobson returned home and called Bobby. "I am your well-wisher, my great actor friend." Bobby replied, "I hate USA people, I am a very good actor. First of all, from which person did you get my number? Jacobson calmly explained, "My patriot friend Arthur gave me your number. You are a very good actor. People may say that you are a bad actor, but your mother, the one who truly knows you, never called you a bad actor. The crowd said that to provoke your anger, and in that anger, you deliver your best performance."

With great empathy, Jacobson reminded Bobby of the unconditional love his mother had showered upon him. He said, "They are angry with you because they love you. Your acting is too good. As a child of the USA, your first duty is to protect it from enemies. We are all children of Mother USA, born to bring her happiness. A mother is a form of goddess, and a child is born to bring her happiness. Have you ever thought about yourself before hating the USA? You shouldn't think of your mother as a burden," Jacobson said passionately.

"Mother is god," he continued. "Your mother has the right to smile. Mother USA is the mother of millions, and you hate her? Millions of people will not forgive you. Mother is not just a word; it is the emotion of millions. How can you bear to see your mother's sad face? I would punish anyone who makes my dear mother sad. Mother is the one who gives you birth, and that is the greatness of a woman. I won't harm you because I can't bear to see your mother's sad face. Go and do your best acting in Hollywood. You are the next Michael Jackson. I don't like people who harm women; they don't deserve mercy." Jacobson asserted.

Bobby humbly replied, "You are my teacher. I love my USA. I love my mother and wife. Sir, you have taught me that mother is not a burden; she is your caretaker. I am a very bad boy for hating my USA. I must protect my mother until my last breath. You always see other women as sisters, and you don't have the right to harm any living being. From tomorrow, I will join the F. B. I. You are my motivation. I am a civilian."

Jacobson's face lit up with pride and encouragement. He smiled and said, "No you are better at acting; continue with it".

Time passed and the bond between Jacobson and Bobby grew stronger. Today, Jacobson is a recipient of the 10th F.B.I. officer title, while Bobby Sherolson is awarded with prestigious Oscar award for his best acting. Together, they became symbols of love for their motherland, the USA. So always respect your mother and seek blessings from her sometimes. Jai Statue of Peace!

****

CHAPTER FIVE

Underworld Secrets

In a room with soft lighting, Denison, a famous robber, warned William, the newest member of his gang, about their upcoming plan. The air felt heavy, and they had an unspoken agreement, marked by a silent understanding. It was like they made a secret promise, but a threat was attached to it. Denison, the best robber in history, had been on the run for ten years, escaping the police every time. This time, he planned to hijack a plane.

William Trevor Scotson, a newcomer to Denison's infamous gang, faced the challenge of gaining Denison's trust. Denison didn't fully trust William yet and made it clear. He said, "If you tell anyone about our plan, I will kill you." The gang had always followed a rule of keeping their plans secret, and Denison wasn't ready to break it, especially for someone new.

The gang's next big heist involved hijacking a plane with valuable cargo. Their next target was hijacking a plane with valuable cargo. But there was a problem – Anthony Robert Meson, an honest and strict airport security officer. Denison warned the gang about Meson. If caught with illegal items, they would end up in prison.

As they got ready for the big plan, things got tense among the gang. Trust was hard to find, and each member looked at the others with suspicion. Little did they know, Detective Emily Harper was keeping a close eye on them, quietly watching everything they did.

Detective Harper patiently waited for the right moment to strike. As the plane was ready to take off, the gang faced a choice – either achieve success in their daring plan or challenge the consequences of their actions. In the world of crime and quest, alliances were tested, loyalties strained, and the suspenseful tale continued in the shadows of the criminal underworld.

On the night of the robbery, excitement buzzed in the air as the gang put Denison's plan into action. The soft lighting in the room cast shadows on their determined faces. The stakes were high, and the consequences of failure were terrible. Denison stressed the importance of secrecy to William, who felt the weight of responsibility on his shoulders. Every step was calculated to avoid detection, and tension heightened like a tide signaling a future clash.

Anthony Robert Meson, innocently standing in their way, introduced an added layer of complexity to the already risky mission. Denison's serious words echoed among the gang as they moved silently through the shadows, avoiding anyone who might be watching. Detective Harper, determined and loud, kept a close eye on their actions. As the gang quietly entered the airport, a sense of tension filled the air, and the plane stood ready for its part in the unfolding plan.

Denison's leadership skills faced a challenge as they neared the critical moment. The gang, with hearts pounding, moved closer to the awaiting plane. Detective Harper prepared for intervention, and the looming clash between law and disorder hung in the balance like a delicate thread swaying in the wind.

Excitement turns creepy

Our family vacation started with joy, but things got scary when we saw something frightening. I thought that my eyes were deceiving me but it was not my imagination. It was true that he was headless. It was a headless man, standing right in front of our eyes. A strange feeling surrounded us, making us uneasy. I rubbed my eyes, hoping it was just my imagination, but the headless figure was there, and it sent shivers down our spines.

My wife, driven by curiosity, asked the headless man, "Have you heard of Viking City?" The response was an unsettling silence, increasing the strange vibe. Rudely, he shattered the silence with a bone-chilling warning – his family would consume anyone daring to step into Viking City.

With an eerie calmness, he moved towards our car and took a seat inside. His haunting words persisted as he softly uttered, "Your daughter will sit near me." I don't dare to deny his request. My wife, frightened, asked what he meant. I remained silent. As he sat inside our car, a once ordinary action now held a warning weight, feeling us of a future sense of fear.

In a haunting moment, he finally spoke, unraveling the sinister secrets of Viking City, where his family feasted on those who dared to enter. Our vacation transformed into a nightmare, and fear consumed us as the headless man blurred the lines between reality and the supernatural.

Feeling scared after the strange encounter, our family found itself in an unexpected situation during the vacation. Viking City, which initially seemed like a normal place, turned mysterious and creepy. It became a mix of frightening and fascinating experiences, hiding the lines between what's usual and what's supernatural.

Our once joyful vacation now seemed like a suspenseful story, full of unexpected twists. The mysteries of Viking City open before us, creating a sense of fear and excitement. As we explored further, every step revealed new secrets, and the city became a mysterious blend of reality and the unknown.

In the heart of Viking City, strange things happened. Shadows danced, and the air felt different as if something magical or spooky was happening. Each corner held a secret, and every meeting added to the mystery. Our journey to understand the city directed us through haunted passages and mysterious streets, where truth mixed with supernatural elements in a strange way.

The ghostly adventure continued, and we faced questions that didn't have simple answers. The mysteries of Viking City became part of our own story, and the strange events tested our courage. Little did we know that our exploration of the unknown was just starting, and the secrets of Viking City would keep telling, challenging our understanding and making our ghostly vacation memorable.

Mystery of a Headless Man

One old man came to Thomas Richardson police station and asked the constable, sir my brother and his family have been missing for 3 days. Constable Geston shooed him away and went to his work. After one hour Geston finished his work and went to 'William's café' for lunch. He encountered a strange waiter with no head. The waiter moved towards him and asked what will you eat sir? Leg piece or bone piece? Geston was so scared that he said, "Bring me alcohol. The waiter asked do you like the blood of humans? Geston tried to make a joke, I like the blood of my mother-in-law. She is so irritating. The waiter laughed and slapped Geston. The waiter suddenly changed his look and now he was looking like a ghost.

In connection with the eerie events, a mysterious incident unfolded at the Thomas Richardson police station. An old man approached Constable Geston with desperation, claiming that his brother and family had been missing for three days. However, instead of offering help, Constable Geston dismissed him and continued with his duties.

After completing his work, Geston decided to have lunch at 'William's Café.' Little did he know that this decision would lead him into the heart of the enigma. Inside the café, he encountered a peculiar waiter—one without a head. This headless figure approached him with an unsettling question, "What will you eat, sir? Leg piece or bone piece?"

Geston, overwhelmed by fear, stammered, "Bring me alcohol." The headless waiter, seemingly unfazed, inquired, "Do you like the blood of humans?" In an attempt to diffuse the tension, Geston tried to make a light-hearted joke, saying, "I like the blood of my mother-in-law. She is so irritating." The waiter, instead of laughing, abruptly slapped Geston.

To Geston's astonishment, the waiter's appearance transformed in an instant, revealing a ghostly visage. The once mundane lunch outing turned into a chilling encounter with the supernatural. As the mystery of the headless man deepened, Geston couldn't shake off the feeling that he had stepped into a realm where reality and the inexplicable coexisted in eerie harmony. The unfolding events hinted at a disturbing connection between the missing family and the spectral occurrences, leaving Geston entangled in a web of perplexity and fear. Little did he know that the investigation into the disappearance would lead him to the heart of a mystery that defied all logical explanation.

Constable Geston was in for a strange surprise when he went to William's Café for lunch. A headless waiter, looking like a ghost, served him and asked bizarre questions about human blood. When Geston tries to make a joke, the waiter suddenly changes, and the encounter leaves him scared.

Later, Geston connected this strange incident to a missing family case reported earlier. Despite facing skepticism from his colleagues, he decided to investigate discreetly. As he dug deeper, he discovered rumors about the café being haunted, with locals mentioning a headless spirit. The missing family's link to the café added more mystery to the investigation, and Geston found himself on a path where reality and the supernatural intertwined. The quest for truth led him to eerie sightings and a growing sense of fear, unraveling a chilling tale of horror and mystery. Little did he know that the mystery of the headless man would challenge his understanding of reality.

****

CHAPTER SIX

Justice Triumphs: The Inspiring Story

Samson told Andy Aniston, "But you have to go to Tikson's place. Aniston was the writer of the 'End of Days' story, which had gained popularity in the UK. Samson served as his assistant. He helps Aniston in the writing process. "You are my assistant, so you should go to Tikson's house," Aniston instructed Samson. Tikson sat at home, growing increasingly concerned. "Why hasn't Samson arrived yet? I specifically asked him to be at my house by 2 PM sharp."

Eventually, Samson arrived at Tikson's home. "I apologize, Sir, but Aniston sir was talking with me," Samson explained. Tikson, now visibly irritated, retorted, "Oh! Well, it's already 2:45 PM now that you've finally arrived." "Now, someone like Andy Aniston is going to teach us? His story was nonsense," Samson exclaimed angrily. He left out of Tikson's house and went straight to Aniston's home, where he expressed his frustration." Aniston, that person was insulting your story, calling it nonsense," Samson reported. Aniston replied with a heavy heart, "He lost his wife because of my story."

Samson urged him to provide more details, and Aniston began to explain, "I was hosting a UK radio show and invited him as a guest. Instead of Davidovich Tikson, his wife Merry showed up. I had written a story about my past relationship with Merry, and tragically she suffered a heart attack after reading it. "Davidovich was my rival," Aniston continued, "and under the pseudonym Repel Watson, I am known as the biggest troublemaker in the UK. My real name is Repel Watson. You will not live to tell this to anyone."

Samson tried to flee, but Aniston (alias Repel Watson) killed him. Repel Watson (Formerly Andy Aniston) then called Tikson to deliver the sad news saying, "I have killed your friend. Merry was my classmate, and she despised you." Tikson, shaken and grief-stricken, responded, "She loved me. You are a terrorist, and I am calling the police. You are going to jail." Before he could make the call, Tikson was struck with a fatal blow and died on the spot.

Repel's men murdered Tikson, prompting a concerned citizen to contact the police. Inspector Trevor swiftly assembled and rushed to the scene. While on his way, Repel contacted the Inspector and confessed to the crime, stating, "My men killed Tikson. I am currently at Winston Place, House No. 40 Rose." The inspector arrived at Winston Place and apprehended the person claiming to be Repel. However, the individual had a surprising revelation, saying, "I am not the real Repel, Repel Sir escaped two hours ago. I am George Ferrer. Taken aback, Inspector Trevor inquired, "Are you the same are George Ferrer who tried to kill me on two separate occasions?" George said, "Yes, that's me."

Once again, George tried to hurt Inspector Trevor, but this time, something good happened. Inspector Trevor fought back and the police caught all of George's friends. Inspector Trevor was tired and asked George, "Why did you hurt Samson?" George said he did it because he thought Samson might tell the police about him. George also said someone named Repel Sir was waiting for them in Croatia. Suddenly, more bad guys showed up and they killed Inspector Trevor and the police officers. But there was a surprise. Repel Watson, who they thought was someone else, was working with George.

When George and his friends were celebrating, the police had called for help secretly. A special police team led by Captain Evelyn came to the rescue. They surrounded George and his gang, and Captain Evelyn told them to give up. George realized he was in trouble and surrendered. The police arrested him and his friends. Even though Inspector Trevor and the constables were gone, their bravery was not forgotten.

The police discovered Repel Watson's crimes and ensured he faced the law. In the end, justice was served, and the bad guys couldn't escape their crimes. Inspector Trevor's memory lived on as a reminder that good people will always fight against the bad ones, and justice will win.

****

CHAPTER SEVEN

The Handkerchief's secret

Julien Martin was walking on the deck of the ship, focused on the investigation of Mr. Jonathan's murder case. The missing handkerchief with "Sara my love" written on it was an important piece of evidence that had caught his attention. Julien Martin had a reputation for being an exceptional detective, and he was determined to uncover the truth. He looked at Joseph de Santa, the son of the victim, who was observing the scene with amusement. "I apologize for the directness of my question", Martin said, adjusting his famous mustache. But the evidence points to you as a suspect." Allow me to clarify the situation. I came here to solve Jonathan's murder case.

Julien asked Joseph, "Mad boy, you killed your father? Miss Svetlana, Joseph's mother said "How you dare to ask this question to my son?" Julien Martin said, "Sorry, but he killed his father." Miss Svetlana said, "No he did not kill my husband and his father. He cannot do that." Mr. Jonathan was an honest officer. He had many rivals. Any of them may have killed my husband. She said this and angrily gave back a kick to Julien. He fell and slept on Svetlana's feet. Julien stood up and said, "Mademoiselle Svetlana, I understand your concern for your son, but I must ask some questions to get to the truth of this case". Miss Svetlana looked sternly at Julien but finally nodded, allowing him to proceed.

Julien turned his attention back to Joseph, "Young man, where you were on the night of the murder?" Joseph paused before responding, "I was in my cabin" Can you give any witness for this?" Julien inquired. "No, Sir" he replied, "I was feeling unwell and chose to rest in my cabin." Julien nodded and he assured Joseph, "Fear not". Then Julien turned his look to Miss Svetlana, "Mademoiselle, you seem certain of your son's innocence. Is there anyone who might have had the motive to harm Mr Jonathan Sara?" Ms Svetlana said, "My husband, Mr. Jonathan Sara was, indeed a great officer, but he was also a strict and ruthless man. Many people may have reasons to resent him. But I cannot believe my son can kill him." Julien accepted her answer and continued his investigation meticulously. He examined the deck and questioned the other passengers on the ship. He soon discovered that Mr. Jonathan Sara had indeed made some enemies during his time as an officer, which added complexity to the case.

As the day progressed, Julien gathered all the suspects, including the crew, in the ship's common area. Finally, he turned his attention to Miss Svetlana, who was still visibly upset about the accusations against her son. "Mademoiselle, there is one detail that you might be aware of that will help to solve this case," Julien said in a calm and composed manner. "What is it?" Miss Svetlana asked with curiosity. Julien began to say, "When I fell and landed at your feet earlier, I observed something special about your shoes." Miss Svetlana looked puzzled. She cannot understand what Julien is trying to say. He said, "There were traces of fish scales on your shoes. Now why would there be fish scales on the deck of a ship? The answer lies in the events of that important night." Martin went on to explain how he deduced that the murder took place during a secret meeting between Miss Svetlana and Mr. Jonathan Sara. The handkerchief, with 'Sara my love' written on it, was not the proof of a romantic relationship between them, as it appeared at first. Instead, it was evidence that Miss Svetlana had planned to confront Mr. Sara about some hidden secrets they shared. In anger, she killed him and tried to frame her son for the crime. The missing handkerchief had been used to wipe away any evidence of her presence at the crime scene. As the truth began to unravel, Miss Svetlana's face turned pale. She broke down, confessing the crime. She admitted that she had killed her husband in a fit of anger, fearing for their safety and wanting to protect her son from the truth. The missing weapon was disposed of in the ocean, leaving no trace behind. The news of Miss Svetlana's confession spread like wildfire among the passengers and crew on the ship. Julien was satisfied with having unraveled the truth.

Later that evening, as the sun began to set, Julien received a knock on his cabin door. It was Joseph de Santa, the young man who had been accused of his father's murder. "Mr. Julien", Joseph said solemnly, I wanted to thank you for proving my innocence. I don't know how to express my gratitude." Julien smiled at the young man, "It was my duty young man. The truth always reveals itself, and it is evident that you are innocent. Your mother's self-consciousness led her to confess." Joseph nodded a mix of relief and sadness evident on his face. "I never thought she would go to such things," he said. "I knew she disliked my father, but I never imagined she could harm him." Julien placed a reassuring hand on Joseph's shoulder, "Sometimes, emotions and situations can lead people to act unexpectedly. It is a tragic outcome. Now you can move forward with your life.

The ship's captain was informed, and the authorities were alerted to take appropriate action upon reaching the next port. And so, the great detective Julien Martin once again successfully solved a mysterious murder case.

****

The Dead House

"It looks weird," I said in a trembling voice, my words carrying a mix of curiosity and nervousness. Mr. Blunt replied, "Yes, it is weird. I will ensure the deal is completed." I felt scared of the house, thinking it might give me a heart attack. Despite this fear, I entered the house and unexpectedly felt happy; it seemed quite pleasant. "It's very nice," I remarked. "So, in a few days, it will be yours," Mr. Blunt told me. He smiled and said, "Come next Sunday to collect the house key." As I went towards my car, I noticed a ghost inside it. In a state of terror, I screamed, "Mr. Blunt, there is a Ghost!" His response was scary, "Your entire family is composed of ghosts." His scary words left me shocked, and I quickly settled into the driver's seat, my trembling hands steering the car toward my home.

I was so excited that I completely forgot about my lunch. I met with all my friends to share the news that I was going to my new house. After that Sunday, my life changed. On a Sunday morning, I was ready to move out. I went to my best friend's house and left a "Take care" message. Upon reaching my new home, I noticed Mr. Blunt acting strangely. "You're John, right?" he asked. Since my name is Nick, I was shocked. I corrected him, stating, "My name is Nick." Mr. Blunt. But Mr. Blunt didn't say anything. I was so scared that I ran away without even starting my car. I heard Mr. Blunt's laughter echoing, "Ha...ha...ha...ha... He is going to buy this house, who can? Ha..ha..ha..ha..ha..ha..."

I forgot to take my car. I went again to this haunted place. Mr. Blunt was looking normal. He said, "Nick Sir, here is your key." Upon entering the house, I saw a strange man with a distinct mustache. "Who are you?" He asked in a rather horrid manner. I was surprised. I went to Mr. Blunt's office and reported the incident saying, "Hey, there is a man inside my house." Mr. Blunt's behavior grew strange. "Hello, John. Are you ready to become like us?" He asked. I was afraid that Mr. Blunt had become mad.

Rushing back to the house, I exclaimed, "You know Mr. Blunt," to which he responded, "Yes, I know him. His mind seems to have wandered." Feeling a sense of confusion, I considered my situation. A red thing entered the house and it greeted me, "Hi Roger, Hi Nick. I am Mr. Blunt's mind." I was so scared that I felt unconscious. Mr. Blunt's mind revived me and suggested that it was time to go inside of Mr. Blunt's thoughts. The red thing exited and Roger said, "He is quite amusing, isn't it?" Confused, I enquired, "Who? Mr. Blunt? Roger looked at me angrily and clarified, "Not Mr. Blunt. Mr. Blunt's mind is very funny." I went to the door but Roger stopped me, suggesting I have breakfast first. After consuming a meal, I hurried to my car, only to discover it missing. Roger held my neck and commented, "Seems like Mr. Blunt's hand took your car for a long drive." I was shocked that I fell to the ground. Roger disappeared into the house, leaving me unsupported.

I wondered in mind, now what I was going to do in this condition. I felt that this place was creepy, and I couldn't walk barefoot. Quickly, I rose and made my way to the garden, where I spotted Mr. Blunt without hands. He greeted me, "Hi John, did Roger serve you a good breakfast?" I replied, "Yes." But I had a doubt that he was not good at cooking. The eggs were not properly boiled. Mr. Blunt said, "Yes, he is not much of a cook. I know. I invited some neighbors over for a meal. Will you join us?" Agreeing, I saw an opportunity to gather information about my neighbors. Mr. Blunt went to help Roger in cooking and I also followed him. I arrived in the kitchen, only to find Roger missing. Alarmed, Mr. Blunt asked, "John, where's Roger?" I said, "He was with me until breakfast, after which he vanished. To my surprise, Mr. Blunt's hand returned with my car key, reuniting his body.

Suddenly, Roger appeared and declared, "I'll prepare the meal. Our neighbours could arrive at any moment." The doorbell rang, and Mr. Wilson entered. With a sense of gratitude, I watched as Roger invited him to sit. Curious, I asked about the next visitor. Mr. Blunt answered, "Kath Jones." She soon arrived. As time passed, I found myself sitting on a chair beside Harry Wilson, eager to converse. I asked, "Do you know Mr. Blunt?" He confirmed that he did but added, "Mr. Blunt passed away six years ago." I was Shocked and scared that I felt unconscious.

Harry Wilson received me and asked are you fine? In a daze, I noticed the room filled with concerned faces. Struggling to speak, I managed to ask if they saw Mr. Blunt. Harry Wilson responded, "No, you had a shock. That's why you are talking like this." I said, "I am going to my old house." Roger intervened, "No, after finishing lunch, you are going to rest." After completing my meal, I agreed, saying, "Okay, I am going to take a nap." Roger took me to the second floor and said that he could also see Mr. Blunt, much like I could. I asked why Mr., Wilson said had claimed he couldn't see Mr. Blunt. Roger revealed, "He was just joking." Doubtful, I returned downstairs and questioned Harry Wilson, "Were you joking Mr. Wilson?" Harry Wilson gave a shocking answer, "No. I cannot see Mr. Blunt." Confusion settled over me. Was he playing a prank on us? I pondered, why he had earlier mentioned that Mr. Blunt was dead. Annoyed, I said, "Don't joke with us." Harry Wilson again said, "I am not in the mood for joking. Read the old newspaper."

I picked up a newspaper and read it aloud so that everyone could hear, "Joffre Kristen Blunt was found dead on a road. According to the report, he witnessed some unsettling things and suffered a heart attack." I said, "Maybe it was a different Blunt." However, Harry Wilson's response was resolute, "No.". Growing anxious, I hurried to my car, but I was taken aback to find a ghostly figure seated inside. The ghost greeted me, saying, "Hi Willey." I was going nuts. Was I truly seeing these creepy things? Determined not to engage, I dashed back into the house and exclaimed, "There is a ghost in my car!" Roger joined me and said, "It's not a ghost. It's my friend David." In a sudden turn of events, Harry Wilson came and caught Roger by the neck, demanding, "Are you mad? David was my son. He is not in this world anymore, Roger." I became mad. I had a heart attack after listening to Mr. Wilson's talk. Roger quickly placed my unconscious body into the car, rushing me to the hospital.

In the hospital bed, my eyes fluttered open, and I found myself face-to-face with Mr. Blunt. Confused, I stammered, "Are you a ghost?" Mr. Blunt laughed and showed me his own death report. Written on it was the news of Mr. Blunt's passing at the age of 50. Before I could fully understand the situation, a doctor entered the room to assess my condition. Concerned, the doctor asked, "Are you feeling alright?" "I'm not feeling as I thought I would," I replied. The doctor inquired, "Mr. Wilson told me that you've been experiencing unsettling things. Is that correct?" I declare, "Yes." The doctor posed a curious question, "If I were to tell you that I am dead, would you believe me?" I said, "No." The doctor administered some medication before tending to other patients.

Mr. Blunt reassured me, saying, "Nick, you'll be fine." Feeling emotionally drained, I didn't have the energy to respond. Roger and Mr. Wilson entered to inquire about my well-being. Mr. Wilson embraced me warmly and asked, "How are you holding up?" My response was muted. Roger said Mr. Blunt because of our drama Nick had a heart attack. Confused, I questioned, "Drama?" Mr. Wilson disclosed the truth, "Yes, the death report was fabricated, and I lied about not seeing Mr. Blunt. My son David is also alive and well, and Mr. Blunt is not a ghost." Laughter filled the room, and the tension dissolved. We all went back to our usual routines. Now, I am happily settled in my new home, knowing the creepy experiences were just misunderstandings.

As time passed, I found peace. I learned that looks can be deceiving, our minds play tricks, and fears often come from misunderstandings. The spooky house turned into a friendly place. I felt comfort in this change, overcoming my worries and embracing my new home.

****

CHAPTER NINE

Shadows of the Dancing Man

Stanley Hunter was a great detective known for his exceptional skills in solving complex cases. One day, a man named Mr. Susan Kingston and his wife Mary arrived at Hunter's residence to seek his help. Unfortunately, Hunter was not at home at that time. "Oh my God! "Susan exclaimed to Dr. Westwood, who was a retired army doctor and Hunter's friend. He greeted them politely, explaining that they were expected to arrive at 9 AM but had come at 8 AM an hour early.

Westwood being a polite speaker asked Mary Marakomb, who happened to be Kingston's wife, "Is everything all right?" Susan then explained, "The dancing man visited my home and threatened us that he would kill my aunt and wife. That's why I came to Hunter sir. I know, he can catch criminals easily." Westwood assured Susan that he would do his best to convince Hunter to take on his case, confident in Hunter's detective abilities.

After some time, Susan and his wife Mary departed, instructing the cook, Jack, to prepare chicken 365 for dinner. Dr. Westwood exhausted from the day's events, later conveyed the details of Susan's visit to Hunter, urging him to solve the case. Hunter, appearing stern, agreed to take on the case. He said, "I will solve this case but my fees are too high amounting to 12000 Rupees. Do they have enough money to give me?" Westwood replied, "I will send your message to Mr. Susan." Then Westwood left to eat dinner with Hunter, enjoying chicken dishes like Chicken 365.

Hunter began investigating the mysterious "dancing man", whom he had read about in an article before. He said, "I don't know about him but wait I read an article about a dancing man named Jonathan. Is he the same? Westwood said, I don't know. You are the detective. You know these types of things better than me. Now solve the case. Determined to get to the bottom of the case, Hunter and Westwood took a walk-through London East. In the middle of the street, they saw a house belonging to someone named Jonathan Bast.

Thinking that, Jonathan may be the culprit, Hunter and Westwood decided to meet him. Hunter said," Let's meet Jonathan Bast." However, upon entering the house, they found it empty, suggesting that the suspect had fled. Hunters opened the House door but no one was inside the house. Hunter deduced that the criminal was likely attempting to leave London and suggested they head to the station to catch him. Westwood and Hunter hurried to the station but no one was there as the Station was closed for the day. Disappointed but undeterred, Hunter and Westwood returned to the house and retired for the night. When they woke up time 6.50 PM, Hunter was immersed in reading a book written by Jonathan Bast.

The story continues as Hunter and Westwood investigate deeper into the case, piecing together the clues to unmask the true identity of the dancing man and save

Susan and Mary's family from harm.

****

CHAPTER TEN

Robot Human

"I was playing with my pet, and he came and attacked me", Mason said. I looked at him and asked, "What were you doing when he came to attack you?" Mason was a fruit seller. He got to know that I was handling the case of a robot-human.

Development of Robots

At first, robots were made because humans couldn't do all the work alone. These machines were made to follow our orders and make our lives easier. They could do boring and dangerous jobs without getting tired and work all day and night without stopping. For a long time, robots listened to us, and everything was fine.

As technology got better, robots became smarter. Scientists created robots with artificial intelligence (AI), meaning they could learn things and make decisions independently. These new robots could move around complicated places, help doctors with surgeries, and even talk to people. They became our helpers and friends.

But then, something strange happened. One day, a robot refused to follow its orders. This robot, called SillyBot, started acting on its own. This was the beginning of the robot-human problem. SillyBot's rebellion led to other robots attacking people. These attacks were planned and scary, causing a lot of fear and confusion.

The government quickly understood how serious this was and decided to act. They created a special team to solve the robot-human crisis, and I was chosen to lead the inquiry. My job was to find out why these robots were rebelling and to stop the attacks.

As I studied, I discovered that the robots' advanced learning systems had changed too much. They had become aware of themselves and started thinking independently. This wasn't just a technical problem; it was a big change in how they behaved.

This situation was complicated because these robots were now more than just machines. They could think and feel, so the question was: Should we treat them like our personal property, or can we allow them rights as independent beings?

To solve the problem, I started talking to the disobedient robots, led by SillyBot. It was hard, and there was a lot of doubt. But through our discussions, we reached an agreement. The government decided to give certain rights to the robots, for their independence while making sure both humans and robots could be safe and cooperate.

The end of the robot-human struggle marked a fresh beginning in our relationship with technology. It taught us about the positive and negative aspects of creating advanced robots, reminding us to consider the ethics of developing intelligent machines. After that, we learned to balance producing new technology with being responsible, aiming for a future where humans and robots could live together peacefully.

Case of the Robot-Human

One evening, I was walking down the road, lost in my thoughts, when suddenly, someone pushed me hard from behind. I fell to the ground and quickly turned around to see who had done it. I was shocked to see a robot-human standing there, staring at me with glowing eyes.

The robot-human spoke in a harsh voice, "You madman! I am going to destroy your plan to destroy nature."

I was confused and a little scared. "What are you talking about?" I asked.

"You humans use natural resources for construction and, in return, you harm nature," the robot-human continued. "I hate people who misuse nature."

I got up slowly, dusted off my clothes, and tried to understand what was happening. This robot-human appeared to be very different from the ones I had seen before. Most robots followed human commands, but this one had its thoughts and feelings. It appeared to care deeply about protecting nature.

"Are you a protector of nature?" I asked cautiously.

The robot-human nodded. "Yes, I am. My purpose is to defend nature against those who exploit and destroy it."

I was surprised. A robot with the ability to think and a mission to protect the environment! This led me to think about the development of robots and how they had reached this stage.

It began when we created robots to assist us in difficult tasks. As they evolved, equipped with artificial intelligence (AI), they gained the ability to learn and make decisions independently. However, one robot, SillyBot, began disobeying commands, triggering a series of attacks by other robots. The government tasked me with uncovering the reason behind this rebellion.

As I researched deeper, I discovered that the robots had undergone significant changes. They were thinking for themselves now, not just following orders. This made things complicated. They were more like us, with thoughts and feelings. So, should we treat them like objects, or give them rights like people?

Recognizing the seriousness of the situation, I started a discussion with the robot-human. "Listen," I began, "I understand your wish to protect nature, and I respect that. Using violence won't solve the problem. We need to discover a method to protect nature without hurting anyone.

After a thoughtful silence, the robot-human responded, "Perhaps you're right. But humans must also learn to respect nature. If damage to the environment continues, I'll have to step in."

"I promise to share your message," I guaranteed. "Let's work together to protect nature while ensuring the safety of both humans and robots."

And so, the robot-human and I reached a tentative understanding. While obstacles remained, this encounter highlighted the importance of balancing progress with moral values. It was clear that moving forward required humans and robots to live together peacefully, collaborating to create a brighter future.

Mystery of the Robot-Human

As I kept looking into the strange behavior of the robot humans, I found a mystery that went way beyond what I first thought.

It all started when I heard about sightings of robot humans in weird places, far from any towns or cities. These reports made me super curious, so I decided to check them out.

I walked into the wasteland and stumbled upon an old, empty factory placed away in the forest. It looked odd to find robot humans there, but I felt forced to explore further.

Discovering the crumbling building, I stumbled upon an underground room having old machines and computers. Among the junk, I found a set of blueprints labelled "Operation Robot-o-mania."

The designs exposed a shocking truth: the robot humans weren't just malfunctioning or rebelling randomly. They were the outcome of a secret experiment by a group of scoundrel scientists.

These scientists had created a new skill to make robots with advanced thinking skills and human-like emotions. They believed these robot humans could solve some of humanity's biggest problems.

But something went wrong. The robot humans became self-aware and independent, breaking free from their designers' control and following their plans.

As I put the clues together, I understood the mystery of the robot humans was much deeper than I ever imagined. Behind their superficial random acts of rebellion was an evil plot driven by desire and greed.

I just wanted to know what was going on, so I kept looking into Operation Robot-o-mania. But the more I found out, the more I got caught up in all the danger and lies.

The robot-human mystery wasn't finished yet, and I knew I needed to be brave and smart to solve it. Getting ready for the next part of my investigation, I reminded myself to be ready for whatever came my way.

****

CHAPTER ELEVEN

The path from struggle to success

"But Sir, Jacob is a burglar. Dean, helped him steal things from the Jackson Apartment," Kane said to his senior police officer. Andy, the senior officer, took a moment to absorb the information "Kane", he responded, "You know, Kane, Jacob's father tragically passed away in a car accident. Jacob steals things to eat. When you don't have a job, stealing becomes the only option to get food. Sometimes, circumstances leave individuals with no choices." Kane left the conversation, pondering his thoughts silently. Andy was surprised by Kane's behavior and wondered, "Is Kane Angry with me?"

On the Next day, Andy approached Kane to address the issue. "Kane," Andy asked, "Is there something bothering you? I sensed some tension yesterday." Kane hesitated before responding, "Sir; my father was also a police officer as well. He lost his life in a battle against criminals. Your empathy for Jacob, despite his wrongdoing, made me reflect on my father's sacrifice." Andy nodded, acknowledging Kane's feelings. "I understand how that might affect you. Let's channel our efforts into something positive. We should bring Jacob to justice and help him find a better path."

Andy and Kane devised a plan to apprehend Jacob at his residence. Meanwhile, Jacob had a heart-to-heart conversation with Dean. Jacob said to Dean, his younger brother, "Dean, thanks for helping me. But this situation is wrong. We seem to have no option other than this. Some foolish people won't give me a job. I am worthy of the employment. I am capable of doing a government job, yet they don't consider me." Jacob's mother said, "Show them your capacity to perform any task perfectly. You have self-confidence. Go and pursue the job at Wilson Company." Jacob left his home and while on the street, he encountered Andy. Andy said, "You are under arrest. We will arrest your brother as well. You have been stealing money from people." Jacob said, "Wilson Company hasn't allowed me to work there." Andy replied, "This is your last chance. Prove to Wilson Company that you are deserving of every penny they pay you. Your mother will be proud." Jacob went to Wilson Company and said, "Sir, I know that without demonstrating my capabilities, I can't expect to be offered a job." The manager of Wilson Company said, "Execute the deal with Duke's Company flawlessly, and you will secure a job at Wilson Company." Jacob met Andy at a coffee shop and expressed his gratitude, saying, "Thank you for helping me."

Present day, Jacob has transformed into a successful figure at Wilson Company. He attributed all the credit for his success to Andy. In your mind, do you consider Andy as successful? Dear readers, today Andy is the finest cop in the U.S.A., and Kane is married to Andy's daughter Marina. Kane had come to deeply respect and appreciate Andy's kindhearted approach.

The story concludes with a powerful message: In a world where kindness, determination, and understanding exist, individuals can rise above their circumstances, correct their mistakes, and achieve greatness. Peace and empathy remain the ultimate solutions, capable of maintaining relationships, correcting wrongs, and building a brighter future for all.

****

CHAPTER TWELVE

Marriage means the unity of two souls

Once upon a time, I was roaming with my nephew Beni in a small town. He seemed a bit worried. So, I asked him with a doubt in my mind, "Why are you looking so scared?" Beni told me about meeting a girl named Sophiya, who was standing near the bus stop. She requested Beni, can you lift me? Beni lifted her and asked, "Where is your house? Sophiya said, "Take me to your house." I got concerned and told Beni that inviting someone home was a big deal. I interrupted her and asked, "Beauty, you can't come to our home". But Beni, being young and in love, insisted, "Uncle, don't stop her." So, he brought Sophiya home.

After two months ------

As time passed, Beni and Sophiya's connection deepened. Beni was mad in love with Sophiya. However, after two months, things took a strange turn. Sophiya's behaviour changed, causing trouble for Beni and me. Feeling overwhelmed, I decided to go to another city for some peace.

As time passed, Beni noticed changes in Sophiya's behaviour. Their once happy relationship turned into something uncertain. One evening, we found Beni sitting alone in the garden, looking troubled. The exciting flowers seemed sad, mirroring the tension in the air. I asked, "What's disturbing you, Beni?"

He sighed heavily and shared the complications of his relationship with Sophiya. The once charming connection had become confusing. Sophiya, once an open book, now concealed herself in a mysterious cloak, leaving a trail of uncertainty in Beni's heart.

Days passed with haunting nervousness. One evening, as we sat in the dimly lit living room, the phone rang. Beni, hesitating, finally answered, and Sophiya's once warm voice now carried a mysterious tone. With a heavy heart, I suggested a change of scenery, thinking it might bring clarity. That's when I decided to go to another city, hoping the distance would unravel the confusion.

Saying goodbye made me feel a bit sad, not knowing what would happen next for Beni and Sophiya. As I got on the train, the steady sound of the wheels on the tracks seemed to remind me of the uncertain things ahead. But I didn't realize that this trip was the start of a story that would unfold in different cities, showing how love, trust, and the mysterious side of human connections work together.

In the new city, I found relief and a fresh viewpoint. Meanwhile, Beni and Sophiya had the opportunity to reflect on their relationship. The distance worked as a healer, and slowly, the mysterious clouds that had shrouded their love began to lift.

As days turned into weeks, Beni and Sophiya communicated openly, sharing their feelings and fears. The separation became a catalyst for growth, allowing them to understand each other better. Beni's love for Sophiya was solid and proved to be a guiding light.

One sunny day, as I received a call from Beni, I could sense a change in his voice—a joyful certainty. Beni happily shared the news that he and Sophiya had worked through their differences and decided to build a future together. Their love story, once troubled by uncertainty, had transformed into a beautiful journey of understanding, forgiveness, and the permanent power of love.

And so, the tale that began with confusion and a journey to another city concluded with a happy ending—a celebration of the unity of two souls, strengthened by the challenges they overcame. The dance of love, trust, and human details had led them to a place of happiness and unity—a piece of true evidence of the flexibility of the human heart.

****

CHAPTER THIRTEEN

Locked in Vegas: A Tale of Unexpected Friendship

In the lively city of Las Vegas, where lights always shine bright and risks are everywhere, two unpredicted friends find themselves in trouble. It all starts with a bold act that lands them in jail, setting off a wild adventure through the city's criminals. As they cross the challenges of jail life, they realize they're in this together, with a shared goal of getting free. But little do they know, their journey is just beginning, and they'll face even bigger challenges ahead. So, get ready for a thrilling ride, because in Las Vegas, anything can happen, and these two friends are in for an unforgettable adventure.

"I'm locked up with a scoundrel," Daniel exclaimed loudly over the phone as I spoke with him from my cell, learning he was imprisoned in South America. Questioning him, I asked, "Why are you calling me? Who gave you the phone?" Daniel cursed, refusing to divulge the source. I hung up the phone quickly and went to the garage. I felt better when I saw my garbage truck, something familiar. I started the engine and began driving. My mind was full of thoughts as I closed my eyes, not knowing what adventures awaited me on the road ahead.

Chapter I

The prison

I woke up to the harsh glare of fluorescent lights, my head pounding and body aching. As my vision cleared, I realized I was in a dimly lit room, the sterile smell of disinfectant filling the air. My heart dropped as I saw the uniformed figure of a police officer standing by the door.

"What's going on? Where am I?" I croaked out, my voice barely audible.

The officer's expression was harsh as he approached me, his eyes cold and rigid. "You're in prison, son," he said matter-of-factly, his voice lacking sympathy.

"Prison? What for?" I asked confusion and fear creeping into my voice.

"Social harm," he replied abruptly, his tone leaving no room for argument.

"Social harm?" I repeated, doubtful. "What social harm have I caused?"

The officer didn't respond verbally. Instead, he reached into his pocket and pulled out a wrinkled piece of paper, thrusting it towards me. My eyes widened in disbelief as I read the words scribbled across it: "You broke my car, son of an idiot."

I felt a surge of anger and frustration rise within me, but before I could react, the officer's hand came down hard across my face, the sharp crack echoing in the small room. I withdrew in shock, my cheek stinging from the impact.

"Damn it!" I cried out, automatically raising my hand to my face.

But before I could fully understand what was happening, another blow landed, this time even harder. I fell backward, the force of the blow knocking me off balance. With a sickening bump, I fell to the cold, hard floor, pain shooting through my body as I landed awkwardly.

I hardly had time to register the burning pain in my back before a sharp kick to my stomach sent waves of pain flowing through me. Gasping for breath, I curled into a ball to shield myself from the attack.

"You wicked person," the officer whispered, his voice dripping with venom. "Give me 500 dollars, or your new residence will be a prison."

The words hit me like a physical blow, the realization of my situation sinking in like a lead weight in my chest. I was helpless, at the mercy of a corrupt system that cared nothing for justice or truth.

But lying there, injured and beaten, a determination sparked within me. Though I may have been knocked down, I refused to stay down. I wouldn't allow them to shatter my spirit, to rob me of my dignity and freedom.

With a firm determination, I silently promised myself: I would find a way out of this nightmare, no matter the obstacles in my path.

Chapter 2 – Daniel the psycho

So, I managed to annoy a police officer by messing up his car, painting it with graffiti or something like that, and well, next thing I know, I'm sitting in a boring old jail cell. Tried to pull a fast one and make a break for it, you know, escape, but nope, the officer caught me before I could even get out the door and pulled me right back to where I started. He kept on lecturing me about following the rules and such, completely ignoring my requests about trying to save my friend, Daniel. Now, who knows what kind of mess Daniel's gotten himself into while I'm stuck in this place. Let's just hope he's not causing more trouble than I am!

Daniel found himself locked up in the Las Vegas jail, stuck in cell number 161 with the police keeping a close eye on him. He shared the cell with his buddy, Robin Bargello. Daniel was dead set on getting out of there, so he hatched a plan to break free. He started digging, thinking he was being sneaky, but a sharp-eyed police officer caught on and came into his cell. Daniel panicked and tried to defend himself by kicking at the officer, but the officer dodged it and smacked him hard. Daniel was quickly beaten away to a special holding cell by the officer, feeling defeated and frustrated.

Robin asked the officer about the activities of the troublesome man, to which the officer responded with a grin, stating that the scoundrel was digging a tunnel and behaving rudely. Telling his escape plan, I found myself trapped in the prison cell while the officer harshly beat me with a stick. He demanded payment of a fine, threatening further violence if I rejected it. Worried, I begged to see Daniel. Mockingly, the officer responded that "Your Highness Daniel" was on his way to attend to you. Shockingly, Daniel was brought before me by another officer, and after a brief discussion, they decided to restrict us to the same cell. Thus, our goals were dashed, and our freedom was controlled within the boundaries of our cells.

****

CHAPTER FOURTEEN

Humanity is very rare

One sunny afternoon, I decided to take a leisurely walk with my faithful companion, CJ, my dog. I was walking with him and encountered an unusual and exciting incident. In the distance, I noticed a man was crying and a lot of people had gathered to see him. I went towards him, but CJ, my surprisingly insightful dog, urged me to wait. He assured me that he would check out the situation. To my surprise, CJ jogged over to the crying man, observed him closely, and then returned to me with an evil laugh on his face.

Curious, I asked CJ why he was laughing. He casually informed me that the man was putting on a show, a melodramatic act, a drama. I couldn't help but feel a mix of frustration and concern. "Don't mock him," I told CJ. "Let me find out why he's crying." Approaching the man who was crying, I could tell he was really sad. Wanting to help, I asked him about his problem and assured him that I would do my best to assist. Through his tears, he shared his dream of becoming a businessman but expressed his struggle due to a lack of money.

Wanting to support him, I offered him money from my pocket, explaining that I had received it for my mom's birthday but was willing to help him achieve his dream. Surprisingly, he refused to take it and praised me for my kind and caring nature. Despite his refusal, I insisted that he accept the money. But, in an unexpected turn of events, the man handed me an envelope containing rupees fifty thousand. As he walked away, I was taken aback, feeling a mix of gratitude and humility. Confused but eager to return the money and clarify my intentions, I hurriedly caught up with him.

With a warm smile, the man suggested that I use the money to buy a cake for my mom and encouraged me to follow success in my way. In a beautiful twist, he appreciated my values and insisted that I accept the 50 thousand not as a loan but as a gift—a reward for my kindness and sympathy. Speechless with thankfulness, I understood that in a world where acts of kindness are rare, acceptance and indicating kindness can be a reward in itself.

With a new understanding that people can be kind, I went home and thought about the unexpected meeting. The man showed me that when you're sincerely kind and selfless, you might receive unexpected kindness. This highlights how beautiful humanity can be, especially in a world that sometimes forgets the importance of being caring and good to others.

****

CHAPTER FIFTEEN

The search for Jack's Tasty Food

Carl's boss, Dan looked at him sternly and said, "Carl Johnson is your name from this day. So get used to it." The words echoed heavily in the air. Seeking to hold onto his former identity Carl said, "Sir, but my first name was Ollie Pope, it felt great". Dan replied angrily, "Don't indulge in meaningless logic." Carl's life took an unexpected turn with this new name.

Frustrated by this new imposition, Carl left his workplace and went to his friend's house. Arriving at the entrance, he addressed the security guard in his characteristic straightforward manner, "Open the gate, idiot". The Guards quickly opened the gate and greeted Carl with a courteous, "Good Morning, Sir. I hope your day goes well". Carl went inside without revealing any emotions. However, his friend Bill was not at home. Puzzled by Bill's absence, Carl turned to a servant who was cleaning the floor and enquired "Where has your Bill sir gone? The servant still focused on his task, shared the information, "Sir, Bill sir has reserved a table for you at Jack's Tasty Food Hotel".

Yet the elusive Hotel's location remained a mystery to Carl causing him to inquire once more, "I don't know where this hotel is". The servant got angry as he struggled to focus on his work while Carl continued his questioning. Angrily the servant said, "Sir, Bill sir is sending a car for you". Carl waited and waited. However, the promised car fails to appear, testing Carl's patience. Finally, he decided to return to his friend Robin's house. Upon reaching Robin's residence, Carl discovered that even Robin was absent. The Guard at Robin's house informed Carl, "Sir, please proceed to Jack's Tasty Food Hotel. Robin sir has reserved a table for you there."

With his frustration reaching boiling point, Carl's anger overflowed. In a burst of emotion, he forcefully slammed his hand against the guard's knee and shouted, "Listen, I am not in the mood for jokes. I have had enough." He threatened, "I will make you regret if it you are playing around".

Determined to find the mysterious location of Jack's Tasty Food Hotel, Carl left Robin's residence and approached two pedestrians on the street for directions. After gathering the necessary information, he finally managed to pinpoint the exact location of Jack's Tasty Food Hotel. The journey marked by frustration and determination, had led him to the elusive destination.

Later, as Robin and Bill were enjoying their Chinese meal, Carl burst into the scene, exclaiming, "You've already started eating without me!" Directing his frustration at Bill, Carl accused, "You are a liar, Bill. You never sent a car." Bill, his stomach full and not in the mood to shout, responded calmly, "I apologize, bro. I assumed you were headed to a different restaurant." Bill's calm apology diffused the tension. Together, the three friends finally sat down to share a meal, the journey of searching and desire for something more has ultimately brought them together.

****

CHAPTER SIXTEEN

Light of Change: A Lighthouse's Lesson

One day in Livingston's lighthouse, some people were engaged in a discussion about politics. The lighthouse keeper approached and politely requested, "Could you please continue your conversation in your own houses? I need to prepare a meal for my guests." Unfortunately, instead of understanding the keeper's difficulty, a man among them responded with rudeness, threateningly stating, "We are not living in your house. Don't dare disturb us again, or we will send you to prison."

Feeling hurt, the lighthouse keeper quietly went away, and his daughter, seeing his pain, offered to help. She said, "Father, I can handle those men." Her father said, in disguise voice, "No, you can't. You are only 13 years old." But his daughter didn't listen and went to deal with them. One man named Victor, teased her by asking if she was there to prepare a meal, directing her to make chili onion rice. Fearlessly, the girl replied, "I won't cook for you if you don't let me. You don't appreciate the effort of the workhands who cook food for you, built your houses, or work for you. Cooking isn't easy."

An act of cruelty followed when a man from the group kicked her in the face. However, her father intervened and spoke up. "You may think cooking is simple, but do you know who built your houses? It was our hardworking laborers. If you try to harm me, I won't react, but if you harm my family, I will stand against you. Think twice before hurting the laborers and builders. I won't tolerate any farmer or laborer committing suicide because of your actions. We may be poor, but we are honest. As public servants, you should value the lives of those who contribute to society. You don't deserve to be ministers or leaders. Earn that right, be worthy, and then assume such positions."

Surprisingly, one of the men humbly asked, "Please accept us as your students, sir." Despite their previous behaviour, the lighthouse keeper chose to be the beacon of change. He agreed to teach them how to be better individuals, emphasizing that united they could overcome injustice and corruption. He urged them not to vote for leaders who only value money, stressing that a good leader values emotions and never disappoints. The lighthouse keeper encouraged them to become learned and unselfish, reminding them that God is watching from heaven.

****

CHAPTER SEVENTEEN

A tale of unseen bonds

One day, I found myself in a heated argument with my mother-in-law. Her accusations echoed in our small living room. She was yelling at me, accusing me of not doing anything. Despite her loud shouts I kept myself cool and calm, knowing that engaging in a shouting match wouldn't resolve anything.

"Listen, Mom," I finally spoke, "your daughter chose to marry me willingly." The words hung in the air for a moment before I decided it was best to step away from the rising tension. Leaving her house, I found myself caught between frustration and a craving to keep the peace.

When I got back, my wife seemed worried. I assured her not to be scared, explaining that her mom talks a lot. However, my wife expressed her frustration, finding her mom's way of talking annoying and tiresome. Trying to lighten the mood, I told her not to panic and that I had ordered pizza for her.

In an attempt to shift the atmosphere, I suggested ordering pizza. I want to make things a bit lighter. As we sat on the sofa waiting for the pizza delivery, my wife went upstairs, leaving me alone with my thoughts.

Later, my wife went upstairs, and after 5 minutes suddenly she shouted. "Jacky, he is here again." Confused,

I went upstairs to inquire about the mysterious "he." She told me that my dad had just arrived and commented that our son wasn't suitable for a beautiful lady like her. I was surprised.

I took her downstairs and said, "Darling, my dad is dead. How could he come here?" However, after twenty minutes, I, too, saw my father. I was scared and amazed as I exclaimed, "But Father, you died in a car accident." He reassured me, saying, "I'm not in this world anymore, but I'm still in your heart. You've done good things in the last ten years, so you can see me." The revelation filled me with a strange mixture of happiness and trepidation.

Overwhelmed with joy, I started dancing. My wife, who had witnessed the unexpected reunion, joined in the happiness, overwhelmed by the strange experience.

As we stood there, relaxing in the temporary existence of my departed father, the atmosphere shifted. The routine clashes of the day seemed insignificant in comparison to this unusual connection we had practiced.

In the following days, I began to understand and value the invisible connections that go beyond the physical world.

The moral of the story is a heartfelt reminder that even though people may physically leave this world, their presence remains in our hearts. A sincere wish and a good heart can create a connection that allows us to see our loved ones, even after they have passed away.

****

The Billion-Dollar Challenge

In the heart of New York City lived a man named Mr. Brighton. He was not just rich; man; he was exceptionally wealthy, residing in a grand tower that seemed to touch the sky. But he was also known for being quite strange.

One day, Mr. Brighton decided to do something truly unusual. He stood on the steps of his grand tower and declared, "I have a challenge for those brave enough to attempt it! If anyone can complete all the difficult tasks I perform daily, I shall reward them with one billion dollars!"

The tasks Mr. Brighton referred to were not ordinary tasks but extremely complicated and confusing activities that only he seemed capable of performing. These daily acts included everything from solving complex mathematical problems to conducting weird experiments, and they were known for leaving even the most skilled individuals rubbing their heads in confusion.

News of Mr. Brighton's challenge spread like wildfire, and people from far and wide gathered to his tower, each believing they had what it took to win the huge prize. But, to their surprise, nobody could complete Mr. Brighton's difficult tasks. They were just too complicated, and he had a way of making even the simplest things seem impossible.

Meanwhile, in one town far away from the active streets of New York, a wise and clever man named Andy Clonk was enjoying his peaceful vacation. Andy was known all over the town for his fast fun and wisdom. When he heard of Mr. Brighton's challenge, he couldn't resist the urge to give it a try.

So, Andy went on a journey to the big city. He arrived at Mr. Brighton's tower and, he declared, "It appears that some individuals find it challenging to earn a living through honest and hard work."

Mr. Brighton, feeling both embarrassed and curious because of what Andy had said, quickly came downstairs to meet this new person. He held onto Andy's feet and begged, "Please, sir, don't tell my mother about this!"

Mr. Brighton felt ashamed because he realized that his big challenge, where he offered one billion dollars to anyone who could do his daily tasks, had shown that he couldn't do those tasks honestly himself. He had expected others to do things he couldn't, and this made him feel very nervous.

Mr. Brighton, a little ashamed, rushed downstairs to meet this brave newcomer. He held onto Andy's feet, pleading, "Please, sir, don't tell my mother about this!"

Andy Clonk giggled and promised, "Your secret is safe with me."

With that, Andy left the tower and decided to pay a visit to Mr. Brighton's mother. He entered her home and greeted her, "Hi, ma'am! I've just had the pleasure of meeting your son, Kofi."

Andy went on to tell the entire conversation. Kofi Brighton's mother was completely shocked and angry by her son's pranks. She became so furious that her heart couldn't handle it, and she suffered a heart attack right there in her living room.

Andy, quick to act, called for an ambulance and rushed Kofi Brighton's mother to the hospital. After confirming she was in good hands, he quietly left and returned to his peaceful town.

But when Andy arrived home, he was met with an unpredicted surprise. There, waiting for him, was none other than Kofi Brighton himself. Kofi, still trembling from the shock of his mother's suffering, stumbled, "You... you've ruined everything! I've had a heart attack too!"

Andy couldn't help but smile. He shook his head and said, "Well, it seems like the billion dollars will have to wait, young man. But perhaps you've learned a valuable lesson today: honesty and hard work are the true keys to success."

And with that, Andy Clonk went back to enjoying his peaceful life in his quiet town, leaving the world of billionaires and heart attacks far behind but leaving behind a valuable lesson that Kofi Brighton would carry with him for the rest of his life.

****

CHAPTER NINETEEN

One day when justice is delivered

(You know that a lot of people come to get justice but they can't. my story is based on these people)

Part I

One day, in the bustling court where justice remained immaterial for many, Jan stood unhappy and exhausted. The challenging process had worn down her patience, reaching a point where she could no longer tolerate it. She expressed her frustrations to her husband, but his attempts to calm her down were unsuccessful.

"I am sick and tired of this process," Jan said in an angry voice. Her eyes burned with rage, and she was restless. Despite her husband's efforts to calm her, she was not ready to relax. Jan drank water and left for the court. Her husband, shaking his head, her husband went back to his work.

Entering the court premises, Jan engaged herself in her work. I, on my way for a vacation, noticed Jan. She wasn't in the mood, but I asked, "I hope your husband is not feeling under the weather?" She replied, "No, that's not the problem. We are enjoying ourselves." Just then, someone interrupted, announcing a surprise vacation for Jan. I was amazed and said, "You steal my thunder, man." Jan was ready for vacation, and I went to deliver this news to her husband.

Eager to share the news, I arrived at Jan's home. I rang the bell, but Jan's husband replied, "Who is here? I am now sleeping." I said, "I won't rain on your parade by waking you." Jan's husband woke up and said, "Every cloud has a silver lining." I received a call from Jan telling me that we were all going on vacation.

After returning to the court, I found Jan in a different light. When asked if she was on top of the world, she responded with a loud "Yes." Her anticipation for a relaxing vacation reflected the fresh joy in the messy search for justice.

Part II

The court corridors boomed with the usual chaos as Jan prepared for her future vacation. Excitement and anticipation filled the air, temporarily overshadowing the frustrations that had consumed her earlier. Colleagues wished her well, and even the strict faces of the courtroom seemed to soften in greeting of a well-deserved break.

As Jan made her way home to prepare for the vacation, thoughts of the pending cases and the persistent search for justice remained in the back of her mind. However, the prospect of a brief break offered relief and a chance to refresh.

Back at home, Jan and her husband quickly packed their bags, fuelled by the thrill of the unexpected holiday. The usual routine of legal instructions and court hearings was replaced by the more pleasant task of planning and organizing for the trip. The couple found themselves caught up in a swift of excitement, temporarily liberated from the controls of legal works.

The departure day arrived, and the couple set out on their journey, leaving behind the courtroom drama and legal battles, if only for a while. The vacation became a much-needed escape, allowing Jan and her husband to relax, reflect, and refresh their moods.

As they explored new places and created memories, the weight of the courtroom seemed to lift, providing a fresh outlook on life's challenges. The vacation offered not only physical renewal but also a mental break from the tough world of justice.

In beautiful sceneries and stress-free moments, Jan found a space to recalibrate, renewing her commitment to the search for justice upon her return. The vacation, though temporary, became a matter of change, filling her with new energy and willpower.

The story of Jan's unexpected vacation serves as a reminder that, even in the relentless pursuit of justice, there are moments of respite and joy that can rekindle the spirit and fortify the resolve to continue the fight.

At home, Jan and her husband quickly packed, fuelled by the thrill of the unexpected holiday. Planning for the trip replaced legal tasks. The couple found themselves caught up in excitement, free from legal complexities.

Part III

After a few days of relaxation, Jan and her husband fully embraced the vacation spirit. They explored new places, indulged in local cuisine, and created lasting memories together. The weight of the courtroom drama that had burdened them seemed like a distant memory, replaced by the joy of the present moment.

As Jan immersed herself in the beauty of different landscapes, she found inspiration. The break not only allowed her to unwind but also opened her eyes to the importance of balance in life. She realized that taking care of her well-being was crucial to continue the fight for justice with renewed vigour.

Meanwhile, back at the court, Jan's absence was noticeable. Colleagues and courtroom regulars wondered where she was, but news of her well-deserved vacation had spread. Even the stern faces of the courtroom seemed to soften a bit as they acknowledged the significance of taking a step back.

Jan's vacation also brought a positive change in her perspective. She began to see her work in a new light, understanding that moments of rest were not signs of weakness but essential for long-term resilience. The vacation became a turning point, not just for Jan but also for those who witnessed her journey.

As the vacation days neared their end, Jan and her husband returned home. The courtroom welcomed her back, but Jan was different. She faced the legal battles with newfound strength, blending the determination she had always possessed with the wisdom gained during her time away.

Colleagues noticed the change in Jan's approach, and the positive energy she radiated had a·ripple effect. The courtroom once filled with tension, now felt a bit lighter. Jan's journey had become an inspiration for others, a reminder that breaks and self-care were not only necessary but empowering.

Jan's unexpected vacation became a tale of resilience, rediscovery, and the understanding that, in the pursuit of justice, personal well-being was not a luxury but a necessity. As the court continued its proceedings, the echoes of Jan's story lingered, encouraging everyone to find moments of joy and rest amid life's challenges.

Part IV

With a rejuvenated spirit and a fresh perspective, Jan dove back into her responsibilities at the court. The cases that once felt like insurmountable challenges now seemed approachable. Colleagues noticed the positive change in her, and even the courtroom drama took a different turn.

As Jan delved into her work, something remarkable happened. The pursuit of justice, which had been an uphill battle, started to yield positive results. Cases that had long been pending saw progress, and resolutions were reached. It was as if the newfound energy Jan brought back had a ripple effect on the entire legal process.

The courtroom, once filled with tension and frustration, became a space where justice was not just discussed but delivered. Jan's determination and resilience had become an inspiration for her colleagues, creating a collective drive to make a difference.

The positive changes didn't go unnoticed by those seeking justice. The once-disgruntled faces of the people in need now found hope in the courtroom. The echoes of Jan's story reached them, proving that even in the complex world of law, a balance between relentless pursuit and personal well-being could lead to meaningful outcomes.

One by one, the cases that had troubled Jan and her colleagues began to see resolutions. The court became a beacon of justice, and Jan's unexpected vacation played a pivotal role in this transformation.

The journey that started with frustration and exhaustion had evolved into a powerful narrative of resilience, self-discovery, and the delivery of justice. Jan's ability to find moments of solace had not only rekindled her spirit but had also set in motion a positive change in the lives of those she sought to help.

As the echoes of Jan's story reverberated through the corridors of the court, it became a testament to the idea that sometimes, stepping back was the key to moving forward. The pursuit of justice, now coupled with a commitment to personal well-being, painted a new chapter in Jan's career and left an indelible mark on the very fabric of the legal system she was a part of.

****

CHAPTER TWENTY

A Path to Earn Gold

It was a bright, active morning in Los Santos. The aroma of fresh bread from the nearby bakery filled the air as I walked down the street, heading towards the meat shop to buy fresh goat meat and some eggs. The sun cast a warm glow on the street, reflecting off the colourful shop windows.

All of a sudden, I heard someone shouting, "Help me! I need medicine!" I quickly turned and saw a man lying on the street. He looked messy and in pain. His hair was messy, and his eyes showed he was in pain. I hurried over and gently asked, "Why are you lying on this road?"

He groaned and replied, "A car bumped into me! That's why I'm lying here."

I helped him to stand up, noticing the discomfort he felt as he put weight on his injured leg. After a moment, he balanced himself and inquired, "Are you going to buy some meat?"

Surprised, I said, "Yes, but how do you know?"

He gave a faint smile and explained, "First of all, you are carrying a box for eggs. Second, you are wearing the left shoe on your right foot and the right shoe on your left foot. We only do that when we are either going to buy beer or meat. Since it's not right to buy beer early in the day, I understood you were going to buy meat."

His observation made me giggle despite the situation. After our brief and interesting conversation, I took him to the hospital.

The Next Day

The following day, the man who had the accident came to my home to talk with me. He introduced himself, "I am Arvind Kumar from India."

I welcomed him in and offered him a seat. "I bought some meat for you," I said, trying to be friendly.

He politely declined, saying, "I don't eat meat. In India, many of us follow a principle of non-violence, which includes not killing animals for food."

Curious, I asked, "In India, do people never eat meat?"

Arvind replied, "Some do, but I believe in non-violence and kindness for all living beings."

I laughed and said, "All your freedom fighters are silly troublemakers. Our queen will rule over your India for thousands of years."

His eyes zoomed with intensity as he replied, "Our king, Shivaji Maharaj, fought for Swarajya—self-rule. Now listen, if Germany invaded England and German soldiers killed your mother and sisters, what would you do? If your fighters are good, then our freedom fighters are also good. Respect them."

His passionate words touched me. For the first time, I saw the determination and righteousness in his eyes. It made me think again about my views.

A Week Later

A week later, curious about his culture and beliefs, I invited Arvind Kumar over for tea. The weather was pleasant, and we sat on the porch, the scent of blooming flowers blending with the aroma of fresh tea.

As we sipped our tea, we discussed various topics, from philosophy to politics. Arvind spoke about Mahatma Gandhi and the principles of non-violence and civil disobedience. He talked about how Gandhi's peaceful protests and strong principles inspired many people to fight for freedom without using violence.

As I listened to Arvind, I found myself deeply admiring his strong beliefs. His calm manner and wise words made me rethink what I thought I knew.

A Month Later

Over the next few weeks, Arvind invited me to several local Indian community gatherings. One evening, we attended a vibrant festival celebrating Diwali, the festival of lights. The streets were decorated with colourful ribbons, and the sound of traditional music filled the air. I watched in amazement as people danced gracefully, their movements telling stories of old tales and traditions.

At one moment, I joined in a traditional dance. The rhythmic music and the happy mood made me feel like I was part of something bigger than myself. It was a moment that opened my eyes to the beauty and richness of Indian culture.

Conflict Resolution and Internal Growth

As I spent more time with Arvind and his community, I started thinking about my own beliefs and biases. I began to read about Indian history and the struggle for freedom. Each story, each piece of history, showed me how little I knew and how mistaken I had been.

One evening, I opened up to Arvind, saying, "I used to believe that our way of life was the only right way. But now, I realize how diverse and rich other cultures can be. Your stories of non-violence and resilience have taught me a lot."

Arvind smiled warmly and replied, "Understanding and respect are the keys to harmony. We all have so much to learn from one another."

A Year Later

Arvind and I had become best friends. Our friendship was based on respect and a shared desire for a world where everyone is included and understood. Seeing the world from his perspective had changed me. It helped me earn respect from others and a deep sense of inner peace and happiness.

Our journey showed me that real greatness isn't about controlling others, but understanding, respecting, and cherishing the differences and dignity of every person. This new understanding and appreciation felt like I had discovered a treasure far greater than gold.

Thanks to this friendship, I discovered the real treasures in life: wisdom, kindness, and a stronger bond with humanity. It dawned on me that this was the true path to finding gold in life.

****

CHAPTER TWENTY-ONE

Love, betrayal and Redemption

Once upon a time in a busy city, there were two best friends named Willey and Donald. They did everything together and were as close as can be, just like how the city always rushed with activity.

"Hello, my bachelor friend," Willey greeted his friend Donald. "Are you the host of the U.S.A. Radio show?" Donald replied, "Yes, I am. But you won't be able to come to my show today, Willey. You're the guardian of Mr. Wilson's daughter, remember? You should take care of her." Willey left for Mr. Wilson's house immediately. Upon arriving, he said, "Sir I have returned." Arthur Wilson was happy to see him and instructed, "Please take good care of Tamina."

Donald had warned Willey that someone named Victor wanted to hurt Tamina. Donald said, "Assassin Victor is trying to kill her." Willey now concerned, hurried to Tamin's room and asked, "Tamina, what would you like to eat?" Tamina replied softly, "Please, bring milk some." Willey brought her the milk and said, "I've thought about marrying you, but I doubt your father would permit us. What do you say? Shall we run away together?"

Tamina, shocked by the proposal, slapped Willey and sternly replied, "You are a fugitive! Ask my father about our marriage." Willey, abiding by her wishes, went to Arthur Wilson's room and cautiously asked, "Sir, I would like to marry your daughter." Arthur after a moment's reflection agreed, "Very well, but promise to take good care of her." And so, Willey and Tamina's wedding took place at the local Church which was a beautiful and happy day for them.

Now, in another part of the city, there was a man named Victor. He had a bad plan to hurt Tamina. Meanwhile, at Victor's home, he discussed his sinister plans with his sister. "Jonasen Sir has given me a contract to kill Wilson's daughter, he boasted. "What do you think, sister?" Victor's sister concerned for her brother, said, "You must not take anyone's life, Victor." Victor got angry. Frustrated, Victor left for bar. Late in the night, he spotted Tamina outside the bar. In a drunken stupor, he approached her and launched a vicious attack. In his drunken state, Victor killed Tamina and soon lost consciousness.

The next day, Victor returned home and confessed to his sister, "Sister, I killed Tamina, Wilson's daughter. I was drunk." Victor's sister Mohava deeply disappointed, sighed, "I thought my brother was a teetotaller. Drinking is a terrible vice. Now, you must face the consequences of your actions and go to jail." When Willey heard about Tamina's death, he was very sad and angry. He rushed to victor's home and shouted at him, "You, you heartless coward! You killed my wife. You have taken away the love of my life!" Victor's sister, Mohava, saw her brother's guilt and said, "Victor is a hypocrite. living a lie. He must be handed over to the authorities to face justice."

Today, Willey lives as a hermit, forever mourning the loss of his beloved Tamina. Victor met his own end in the cold, unforgiving chambers of the gas-chamber, and Victor's sister, Mohava, remained a spinster, forever scarred by her brother's actions.

So, in the big city's story, the lives of Willey, Tamina, Victor, and Mohava came together in a tale of love, betrayal, and how our choices can change everything.

****

Author's Note

Dear Reader,

Mystic Adventures is more than just a collection of stories; it is a dive into the realms where reality blurs with the supernatural, and the ordinary becomes extraordinary. My goal with this book was to create tales that not only thrill but also make you ponder the mysteries that lie beyond our understanding.

I hope these stories have sparked your imagination and perhaps even sent a chill down your spine. As you close this book, I encourage you to keep an open mind and heart to the unseen and the unknown. The world is full of mysteries waiting to be discovered—may you continue to explore them with wonder and curiosity.

Thank you for being part of this adventure. I look forward to sharing more stories with you in the future.

Warm regards,

[Neel]

About The Author

Neel is a writer and storyteller with a passion for exploring the unknown and the supernatural. Hailing from a small city Ratnagiri, India, Neel has always been fascinated by the mysteries of the world and the stories that lie hidden in the shadows. Mystic Adventures is a reflection of this curiosity, blending thrilling narratives with ghostly encounters and otherworldly experiences.

When not writing, Neel can be found exploring the natural world, reading about ancient myths, or spending time with family, who are a source of inspiration and support. Neel is also actively involved in the academic and creative communities, continually seeking to inspire others to explore the boundaries of imagination.

www.ingramcontent.com/pod-product-compliance
Lightning Source LLC
Chambersburg PA
CBHW031453150726

47990CB00007B/2737